Go Away!

By Janine Amos and Annabel Spenceley
Consultant Rachael Underwood

CHERRYTREE BOOKS

A CHERRYTREE BOOK

This edition first published in 2007
by Cherrytree Books, part of
The Evans Publishing Group
2A Portman Mansions
Chiltern Street
London
W1U 6NR

© Evans Brothers Limited 2007

Printed in China

British Library Cataloguing in Publication Data.
Amos, Janine
 Go away!. - (Good friends)
 1. Sharing - Pictorial works - Juvenile fiction
 2. Children's stories - Pictorial works
 I. Title II. Spenceley, Annabel III. Underwood, Rachael
 823.9'14[J]

ISBN 1842344285
13 digit ISBN 978 1842344286

CREDITS
Editor: Louise John
Designer: D.R.ink
Photography: Gareth Boden
Production: Jenny Mulvanny
Based on the original edition of Go Away! published in 1999

With thanks to our models:
Grandma's Story
Jill Sharpe, Lucy and Matthew Battersby and Amelia John
The Shop
Elizabeth Deller, Ellie Carter and Louise John

VISIT OUR WEBSITE
www.evansbooks.co.uk
Evans

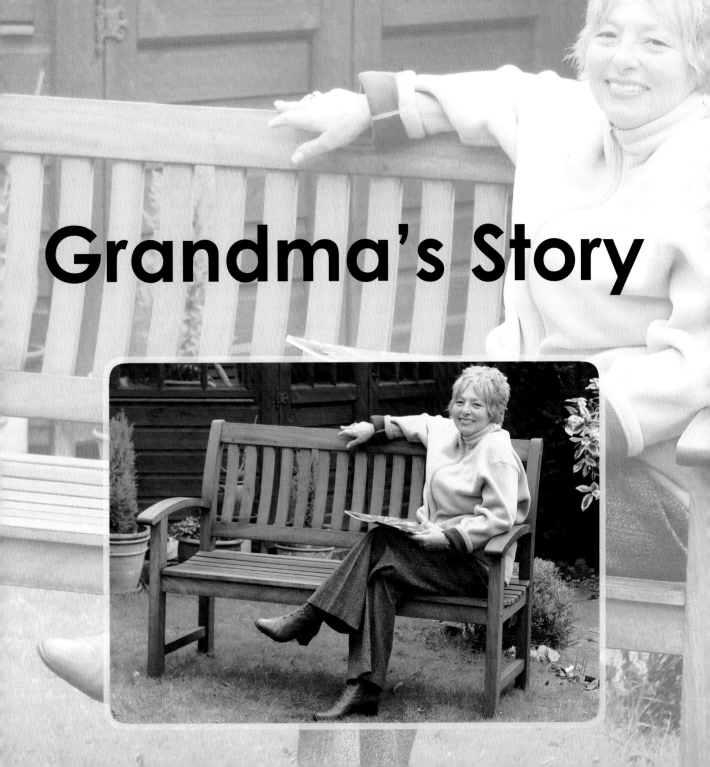

Grandma's Story

Lucy is looking for bugs.

Grandma is reading a story.

Lucy looks up and wants to join in. She goes over to Grandma.

She crawls onto
Grandma's lap
and pushes
Matthew and
Amelia away.

"Go away!" shouts Matthew.

How do you think
Lucy feels?

"Matthew, I think Lucy wants to listen, too," says Grandma.

"But she shouldn't push," says Matthew.

Lucy nods. "I'm sorry," she says.

"What could we do?"
asks Grandma.

**What do you think
they could do?**

"Amelia and I can move over and Lucy can sit in between us," says Matthew.

"Yes!" says Lucy.

"Now everyone can see the book!" laughs Grandma.

The Shop

Elizabeth is playing shop. She puts all the food on the table.

Here comes Ellie. "I'll be the shopkeeper," she says. "You can buy my things."

"Look," says Ellie.
"We can use this money."

"Go away!" shouts Elizabeth.

Mum comes over.
"Elizabeth you sound
upset," she says.
"What's the matter?"

"Ellie wants to be the shopkeeper – and I'm the shopkeeper!" says Elizabeth.

"But I want to sell things too!" says Ellie. "Hmm," says Mum. "So you both want to be shopkeepers?"

"Yes," agrees Elizabeth. Ellie nods.

What do you think they could do?

"I know!" says
Elizabeth. "We
can have two
shopkeepers!"

"But who will be the customer?" wonders Ellie.

Elizabeth looks at Ellie.
Ellie looks at Elizabeth.

They both look
at Mum.

"Mum can!" they shout together.

TEACHER'S NOTES

By reading these books with young children and inviting them to answer the questions posed in the text, the children can actively work towards aspects of the PSHE and Citizenship curriculum.

Develop confidence and responsibility and making the most of their abilities by
• recognising what they like and dislike, what is fair and unfair and what is right and wrong
• to share their opinions on things that matter to them and explain their views
• to recognise, name and deal with their feelings in a positive way

Develop good relationships and respecting the differences between people
• to recognise how their behaviour affects others
• to listen to other people and play and work co-operatively
• to identify and respect the difference and similarities between people

By using some simple follow up and extension activities, children can also work towards

Citizenship KS1
• to recognise choices that they can make and recognise the difference between right and wrong
• to realise that people and living things have needs, and that they have a responsibility to meet them
• that family and friends should care for each other

EXTENSION ACTIVITY
A game
• Read through the first story in *Go Away!* Ask the children the questions posed on pages 9 and 13. Do they think Matthew was wrong to tell Lucy to *go away*? At the end of the story ask the children if they think the problem was resolved in the best way? How else could it have been sorted out?
• Sit the children in groups of two facing each another. Introduce a game to help the children to remember not to tell other people to *go away!* The first child has to think of a situation where he/she might want to tell someone to *go away!* i.e. 'I'm reading my book and my sister disturbs me. I tell her to *go away*.' The child's partner has to try to think of a better way of dealing with the situation than saying go away! i.e. 'I tell my sister that I am busy at the moment, but that I will play with her soon.' The groups take it in turns to stand up and act out the two different versions of their situation.

These activities can be repeated on subsequent days using the other story in the book or with other stories in the series.